To order additional copies of this book, contact:
Xlibris
1-888-795-4274
www.Xlibris.com
Orders@Xlibris.com

HEROES 2011 COMICS

TEN MINUTES LATER SCOTT HEARD SOMETHING DANGEROUS WITH HIS TURBO HEARING.

I'M MORE THAN JUST AN MAN! I'M A PART MACHINE AN STEEL THATS A GOD! I WILL DEFEAT YOU TURBO-MAN!

THEN TWO-GUNS TRANFARM HIMSELF INTO A MACHINE GOD!

5

TURBO-MAN WAS GETTING WEAKER AND WEAKER BY TWO-GUNS POWER.

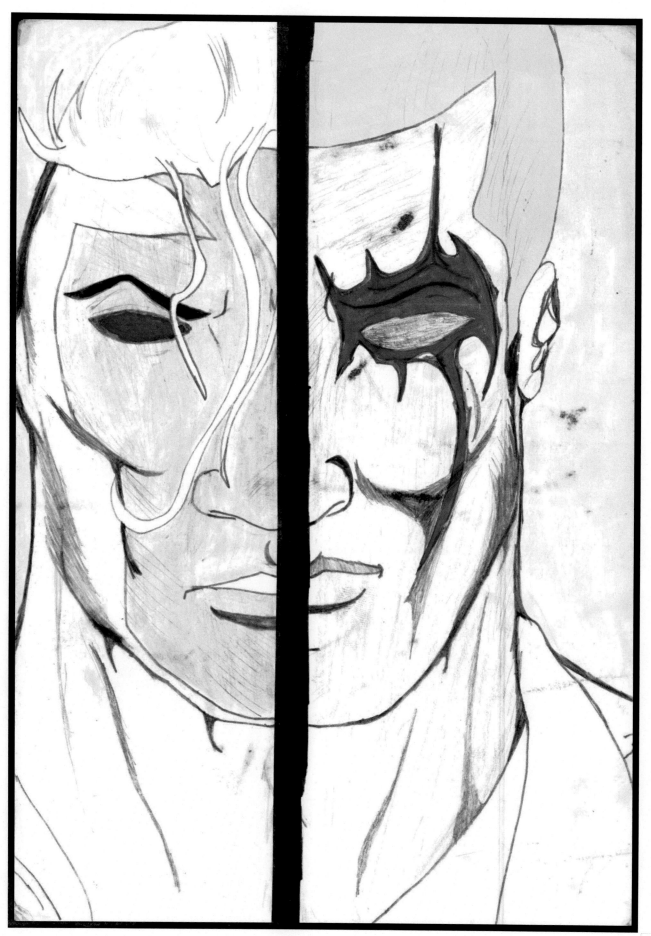

13

15

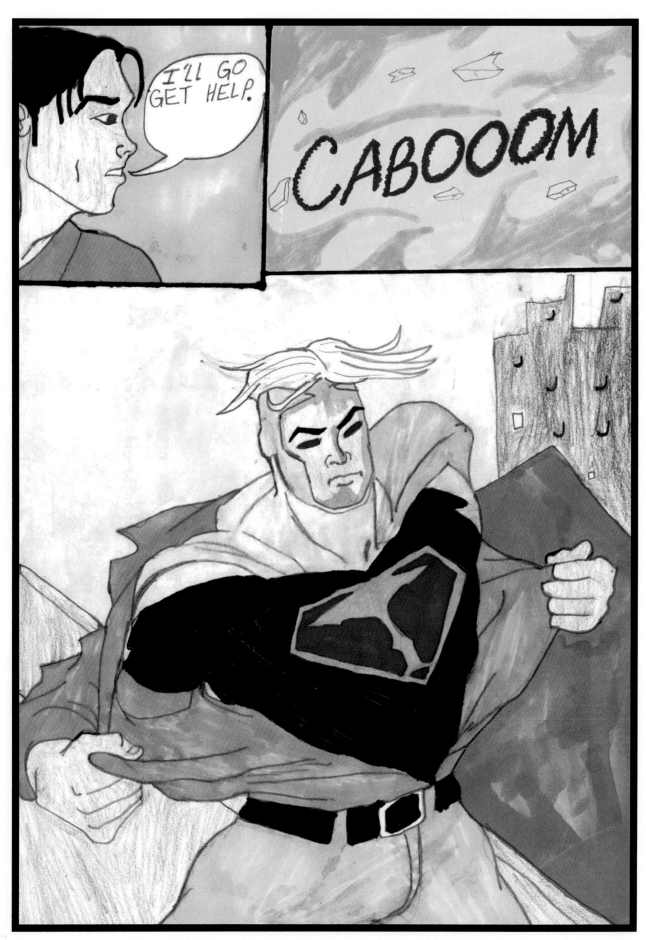

17

19

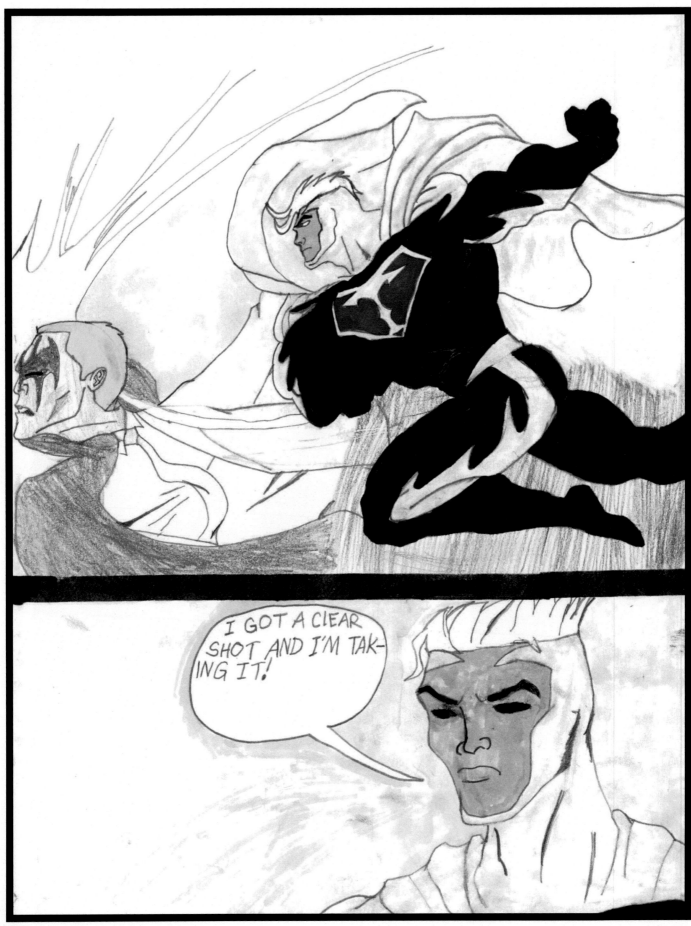

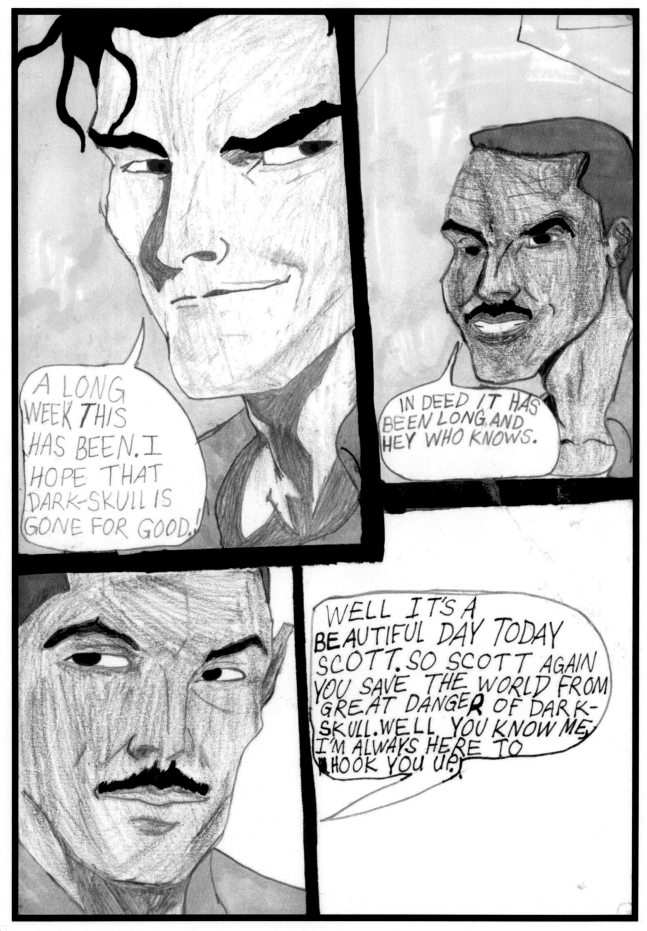

23

TURBOMAN

REAL NAME: SCOTT AUSTIN
DUAL IDENTITY: SECRET
HEIGHT: 6'1"   WEIGHT: 201
EYES: BLUE   HAIR: BLACK
OCCUPATION: WAREHOUSE
FORMER OCCUPATION: MANAGER
PLACE OF BIRTH: MIAMI
FLORIDA

MARITAL STATUS:
SINGLE/GIRLFRIEND

SUPERHUMAN
POWERS:
FLYING TURBO
SPEED, TURBO
SPEAR, A
TITAN,
BULLET PROOF,
SURE R TURBO
VISION,
SUPER STRENGTH
X-RAY TURBO
VISION,
TURBO SENCE

WEAPONS: NONE

HEROES 2011 COMICS